To Sonali F, who inspired me,
and Karen G, who believed in me.
—ES

To my daughter, Luce,
my little ray of sunshine
—LF

little bee books

A division of Bonnier Publishing
853 Broadway, New York, New York 10003
Text copyright © 2016 by Erica Silverman
Illustrations copyright © 2016 by Laure Fournier
Manufactured in China   LEO 0516
First Edition 10 9 8 7 6 5 4 3 2 1
Library of Congress Cataloging-in-Publication data is available upon request.
ISBN 978-1-4998-0173-6
littlebeebooks.com
bonnierpublishing.com

WAKE UP, CITY!

by
Erica Silverman

illustrated by
Laure Fournier

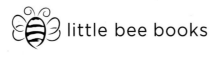
little bee books

My city sleeps, but we're awake
in the quiet time before daybreak.

When Daddy whispers, "It's time to go,"
we set off in the street lamps' hazy glow.

Like giant statues, tall trees doze,
and rows of cars sleep tail to nose.

A cat is curled up in a loop,
yawning as we pass her stoop.

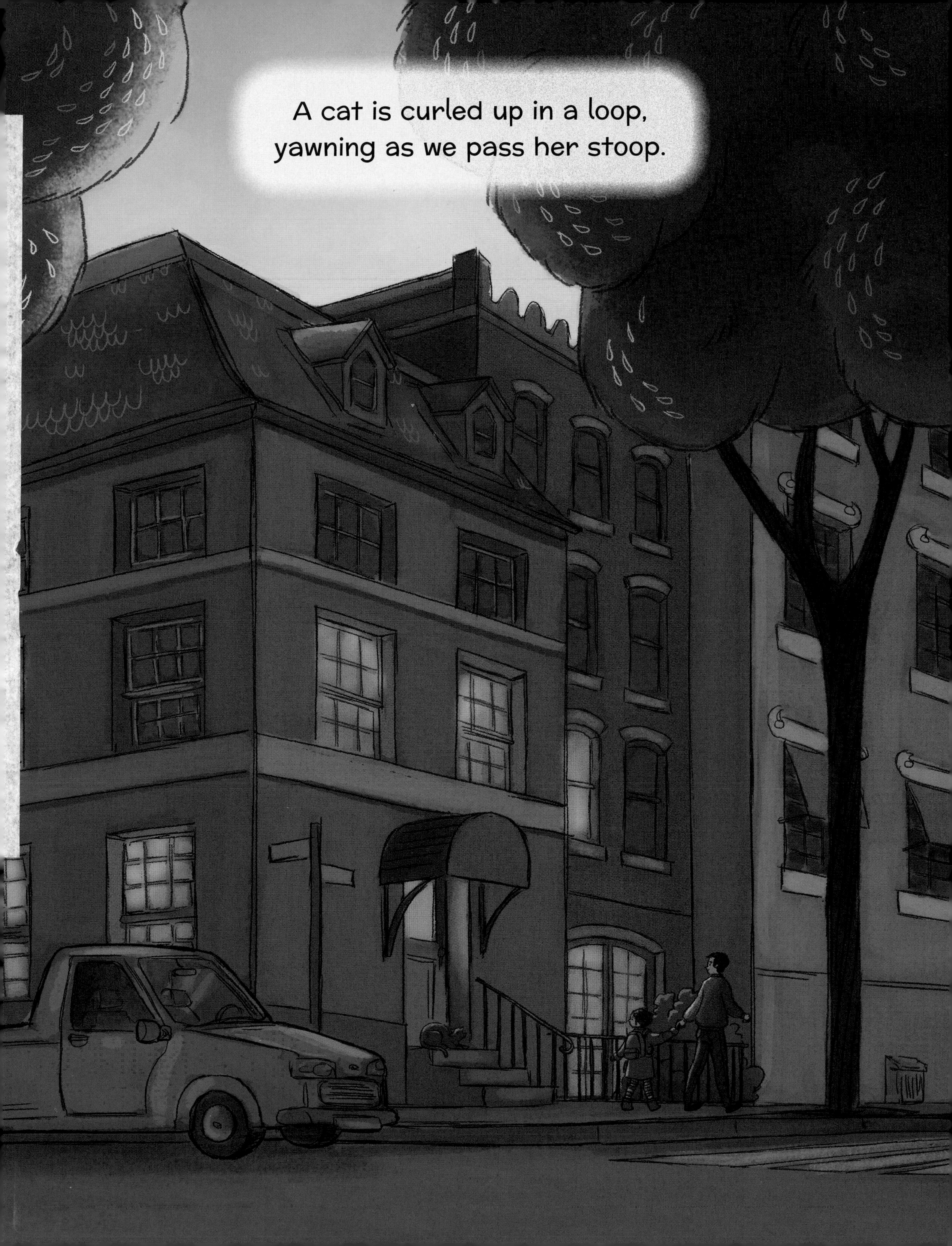

Empty benches in the park
look lonely in the fading dark.

No one rides the waiting swings.
I count five pigeons with tucked-in wings.

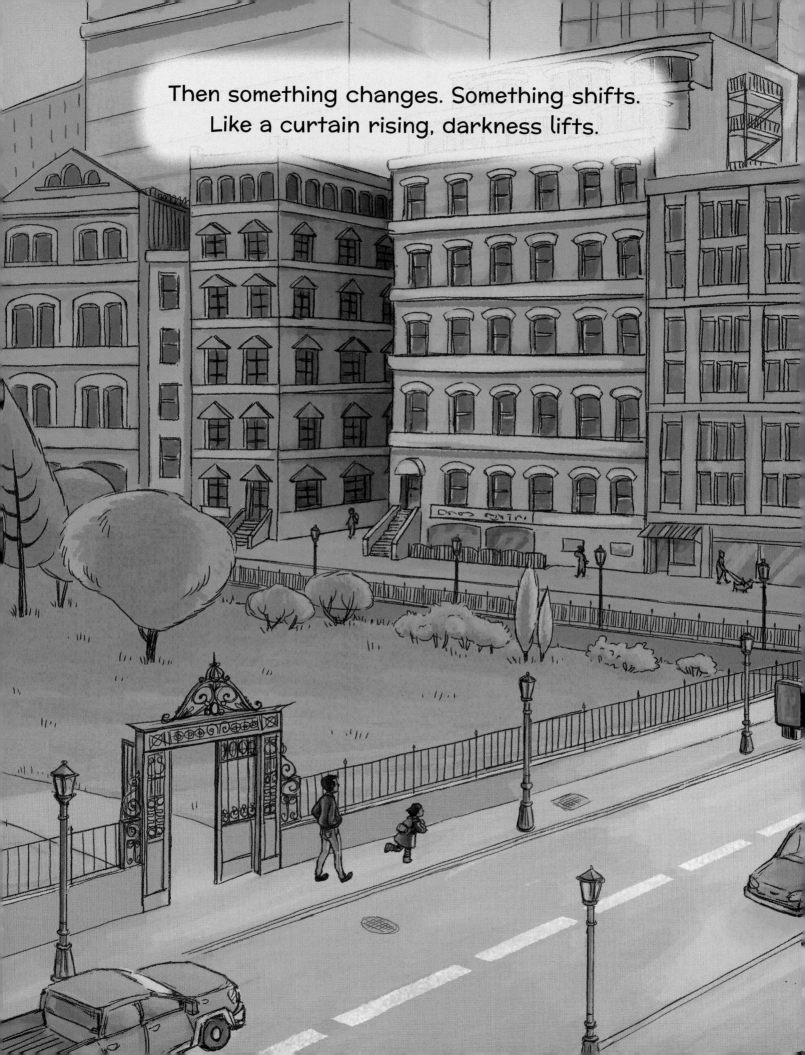

Then something changes. Something shifts.
Like a curtain rising, darkness lifts.

Look around! It's growing light.
Wake up, city! Good-bye, night!

The gumdrop sun rises high
in the cotton candy sky.

A woman stretches. She starts to run.
The city morning has begun!

Here comes a beast on hairy feet, whooshing, swooshing down the street.

Swoosh-ah! Swoosh-ah!
Brushes sweep!
The driver waves and gives a beep.

And now the rumbling garbage truck stops to empty bins of muck.

It tilts one over, dropping glop,
and fills its belly with smelly slop.

Store gates roll up. Clatter! Clang!
Van doors open with a bang.

Out come apples, yams, and beets,
and trays of doughnuts that smell so sweet!

It's bright and busy at the gym.
But the toy store's closed; its lights are dim.

Inside the fish mart, ice chips gleam,
and the pretzel cart makes clouds of steam.

They gather carrots in a crate.
Daddy says, "Come on, we're late!"

I stop to watch the drill machine,
but then the traffic light turns green.

Time is flying—tick tick tock!
Hurry! Hurry! One more block!